Copyright © 2020 Clavis Publishing Inc., New York

Originally published as *Winter met Fien en Milo* in Belgium and the Netherlands by Clavis Uitgeverij, 2019
English translation from the Dutch by Clavis Publishing Inc., New York

Visit us on the Web at www.clavis-publishing.com.

Winter with Lily and Milo written and illustrated by Pauline Oud

ISBN 978-1-60537-565-6

This book was printed in July 2020 at Wai Man Book Binding (China) Ltd.
Flat A, 9/F., Phase 1, Kwun Tong Industrial Centre, 472-484 Kwun Tong Road, Kwun Tong, Kowloon, H.K.

First Edition
10 9 8 7 6 5 4 3 2 1

Clavis Publishing supports the First Amendment and celebrates the right to read.

Extra materials available at www.paulinespreschoolproject.com

Winter with
Lily and Milo

Pauline Oud

It's winter!
Lily and Milo are going outside.
They want to feed the birds
in the yard.

What will Lily and Milo wear?
A winter coat or a bathing suit?
Will they wear warm hats?
Do they put on mittens and maybe a scarf?
And how about flip-flops or warm boots?

It's much too cold for a bathing suit!
Lily and Milo each put on a winter coat.
And their mittens and boots.
The scarf and hat help keep them warm too.

What will they take with them?
They bring delicious apples and some string.
And also a bag of seeds and a garland of peanuts.
But how will they carry these things?
In the blue cart or in the handbag?

Lily and Milo take everything in their cart.
Brrrr—it's really cold outside!

Look—the pond is frozen.
Oops! Careful, Milo. Don't slip!

The trees are bare. The ground is frozen.
The birds can't find any food in the yard.
Luckily Lily and Milo are here to help.

Lily hangs the apples and the garland of peanuts in the tree. Milo sprinkles the seeds in the bird feeder. The birds are so happy!

Hey, what's that?
White flecks fall from the sky.
The flecks are cold, and wet, and white . . .

It's snow!
Everything is turning white.
"Hooray," Lily and Milo cheer. "It's snowing!"

Later, Lily and Milo play in the snow.
They sled down the hill.
Whee! The snow is slippery and soft.

Lily starts to roll a big ball of snow.
"Will you give me a hand?" Lily asks.
Milo makes a ball too.

What are Lily and Milo making?

It's a snowman!

Brrrr . . . Milo is cold.
"Where is your scarf?" Lily asks.
"And your hat?"
Milo doesn't know.
And his mittens are missing too.

Lily and Milo search everywhere.
But they can't find Milo's mittens,
scarf, or hat.
"C-c-old," Milo shivers.

"Let's go inside," says Lily.
"It's much too cold for you now."
"But the snowman isn't done yet!" says Milo.

At home Lily stomps her feet to clean her boots.
Now the mat is covered in snow!
It's so warm inside, the snow is melting on the floor.

Lily is making soup for Milo.
She takes out bowls and spoons.
"I have soup to warm you up, Milo.
Milo . . . Milo? Where are you?"

Milo is outside finishing the snowman!

It's getting dark outside.
Bye, snowman! Bye, snow! Bye, birds!
Such a lovely winter's day!